THIS BOOK BELONGS TO:

_____

_____

_____

First U.S. paperback edition 2007

Library of Congress Cataloging-in-Publication Data is available.

Library of Congress Catalog Card Number 2004057468

ISBN 978-0-7636-3504-6 (hardcover)
ISBN 978-0-7636-9973-4 (paperback)

18 19 20 21 22 23 APS 10 9 8 7 6 5 4 3 2 1

Printed in Humen, Dongguan, China

This book was typeset in Bembo.
The illustrations were done in colored pencil.

Candlewick Press
99 Dover Street
Somerille, Massachusetts 02144

visit us at www.candlewick.com

Mr. Large in Charge

Jill Murphy

CANDLEWICK PRESS

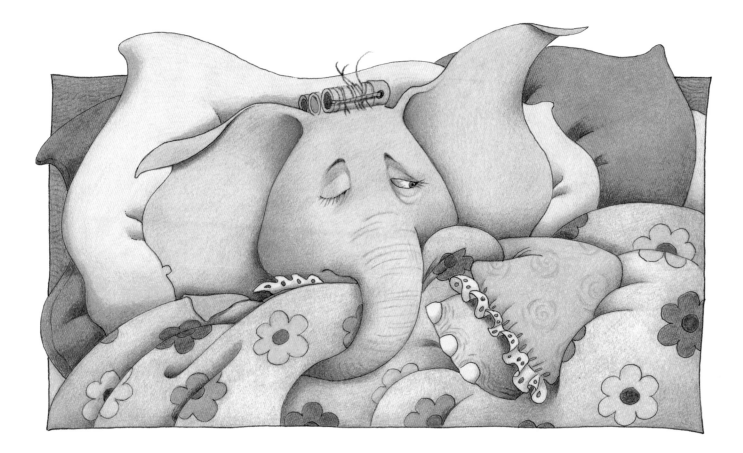

Mrs. Large opened one eye and peered out at the morning. She forced open the other eye, dragged herself out of bed, and set off downstairs to the kitchen, where Mr. Large had kindly started the children on their breakfasts.

"You look awful, dear," said Mr. Large.

"Don't say that to Mommy!" said Laura indignantly.

"Mommy looks beautiful!" exclaimed Lester.

"Boo'ful Mommy," cooed the baby.

"Yes, of course Mommy's beautiful," said Mr. Large.

"I meant she doesn't look *well*—are you feeling
all right, dear?"

"As a matter of fact, I *don't* feel too good,"  admitted Mrs. Large. "But I was going to take the children to the park later on. Then there's the shopping and the lunch and there's—"

"Well, you don't have to worry about any of that," said Mr. Large. "It's the weekend, so I'm in charge. Go on, back to bed with you—we'll take care of everything, won't we, kids?"

"You bet!" yelled Lester.

Mrs. Large trudged back upstairs clutching a
nice hot-water bottle and sank back into the
bed, which was still warm.
"What a treat!" she said.

Downstairs, Mr. Large was organizing his troops.

"Right, men!" he commanded.

"We're not *all* men," said Laura.

"Oh, you know what I mean," said Mr. Large.

"Well, troops, then—all right?

"I'll take the worst task—that's doing the dishes.

"Lester, you tackle the vacuuming; Luke, picking things up off the floor; Laura and the baby, general dusting and cushion-plumping. Quick march. One-two, one-two, off you go."

Mr. Large turned on the radio, found a cheery tune to get everyone going, and soon they were all busy with their tasks.

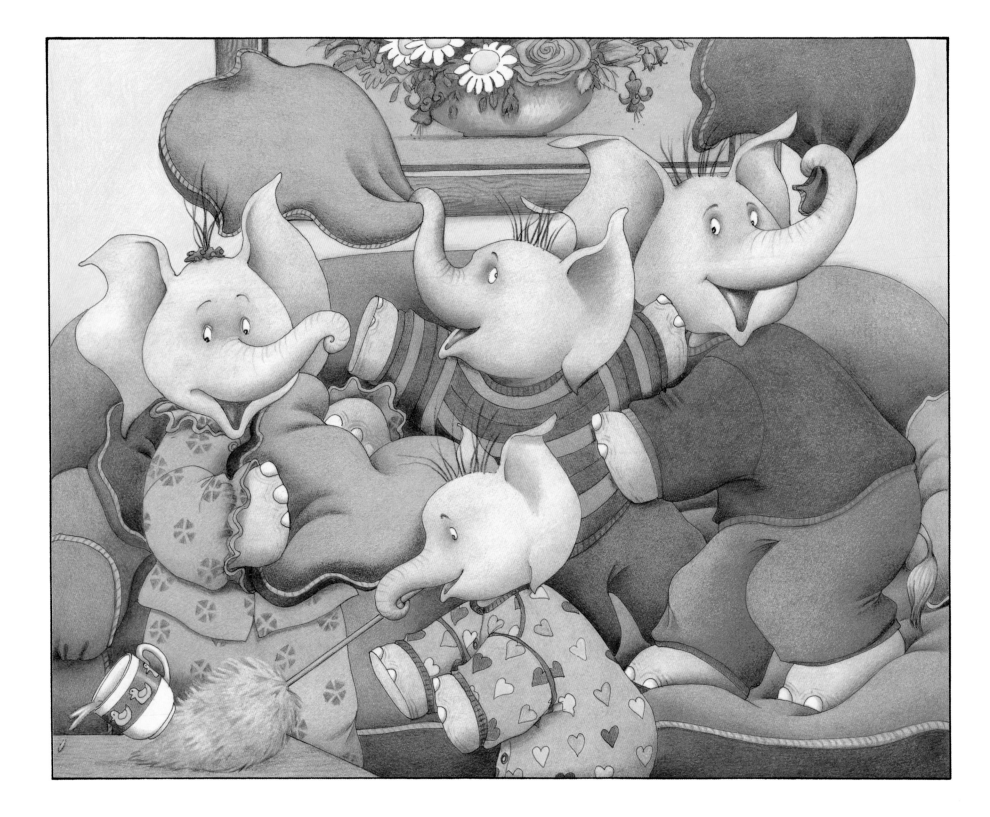

Upstairs, Mrs. Large was jolted back from the brink of
sleep by the astonishing amount of noise blasting up
through the floor. She listened anxiously for a while,
but could soon tell they were mostly happy noises,
so she wedged a pillow around her ears and decided
to ignore it.

Mrs. Large had just drifted off to sleep when
she was startled awake by the baby, who was
giving her a thorough dusting.

"Sorry, Mom!" yelled Laura, rushing in
and grabbing the baby.

The baby began to scream and hung on to
the covers so that they both
fell over backward.

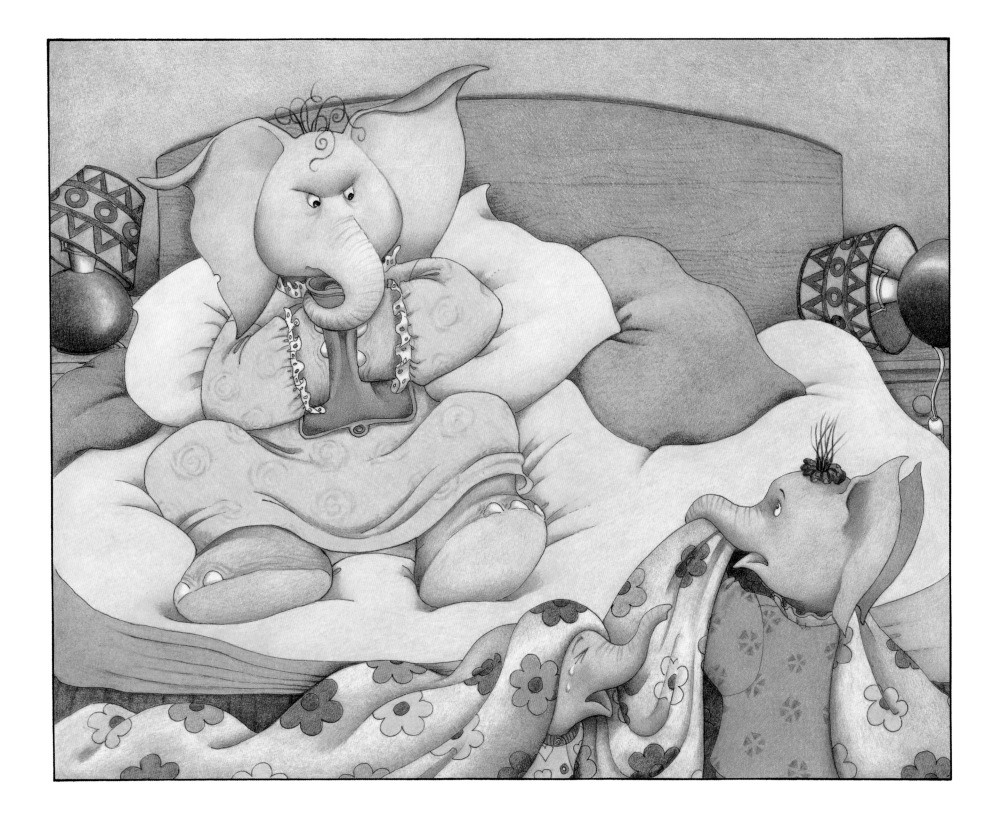

"This isn't proving very restful, Laura," said Mrs. Large crossly as Laura disentangled herself and the baby and attempted to bundle the covers back onto the bed.

"Mommy, huggy!" screamed the baby.

"WANT MY MOMMY! BIG HUGGY NOW!" Laura stuffed the baby under her arm and wrestled her out the door. "Don't worry, Mom," she called as she closed the door behind them.

"I'll take her down to Dad."

"Don't want Dad," bellowed the baby.

"Want Mom! WANT MY MOMMY!"

Mrs. Large rearranged the mangled covers and snuggled down, feeling decidedly jangled. Suddenly there was an almighty crunch from downstairs, and the vacuum stopped abruptly.

The bedroom door opened,
and Lester looked in.
"It's all right, Mom!" he
reassured her. "Nothing broke—
it just *sounded* bad."
Luke's head appeared around
Lester's knees.
"That's right, Mom!" he agreed.
"Nothing to worry about.
You just go back to sleep—
everything's under control."

Mrs. Large was finally dropping off when Mr. Large crashed open the bedroom door.

"We're all off to the park now, dear," he announced. "We'll do the shopping on the way home. Then we can bring you up a nice lunch."

"Thank you, dear," said Mrs. Large. "I'm having a lovely rest." Mr. Large beamed and blew his wife a kiss as he backed out of the room, closing the door *very quietly*.

At last, Mrs. Large dozed off. What seemed like five minutes later, she was awoken by a smell of burning. Just then, Laura put her head around the door. "Dad says not to worry about the smell," she said. "He's getting lunch, and he wants to know if you'd like some."

"What exactly *is* it?" asked Mrs. Large nervously.

"Well," said Laura, "it *was* something in a special sauce, but Dad just had a little peek at the soccer game on TV—well, it was quite a long peek actually. So now it's cheese sandwiches."

"I think I'll keep on sleeping. Thank you, dear," said Mrs. Large. "Perhaps I could join you for a snack later."
"Okay," said Laura, slamming the door as she rushed off to tell Dad.

Mrs. Large closed her eyes and tried to relax.

What seemed like three seconds later, the door crashed open again, and all the children came charging in.

"We're going to play soccer with Dad!" yelled Lester.

"In the yard!" said Luke.

"Now!" said the baby.

"Are you feeling a *bit* better?" asked Laura.

"Mommy better?" asked the baby. "Big huggy?"

"A *bit* better," said Mrs. Large. "You go and have fun with Daddy, and perhaps I'll be all right later on."

"Big, BIG huggy!" wailed the baby as Lester scooped her up and carried her out. "Big huggy, Mommy. NOW!"

"Don't worry, Mom," said Laura. "She loves soccer once she gets going!"

The door slammed shut for the hundredth time.

Mrs. Large winced and slithered down under the covers.

Joyful sounds came drifting in from the yard,

and Mrs. Large smiled contentedly.

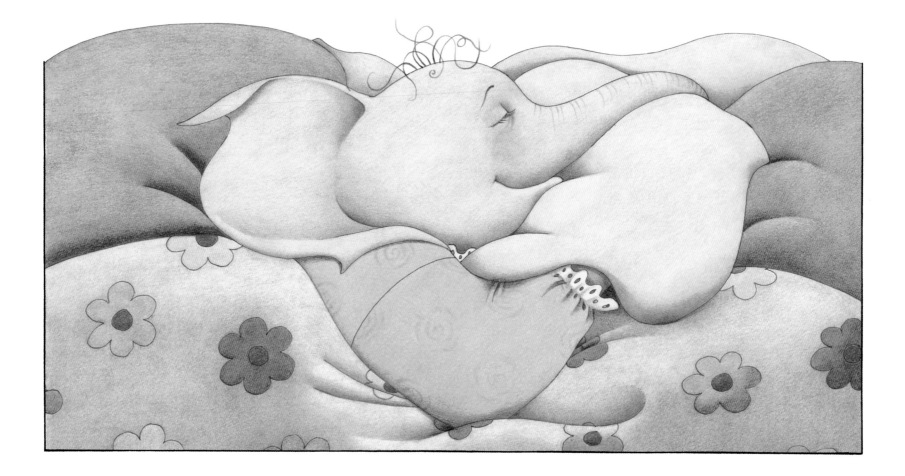

Five minutes later, Lester burst into the bedroom.
"Dad wants to know where the bandages are!" he yelled.
"Don't worry, Mom—it's not the baby. Dad tripped over
the rake."

"They're on top of the
bathroom cabinet,"
said Mrs. Large weakly.

After a while, the door opened again, and Mr. Large
came in carrying a tray laden with food.
The children sneaked in behind him and lurked.
The baby didn't lurk for long. She climbed grimly
onto the bed and clasped her mother around the neck.
"Big huggy," she crooned.

"Everyone out!" ordered Mr. Large.
"Let Mommy have her rest
now. She's not well today."
Mrs. Large heaved herself
into a sitting position and
patted the covers.
"That's all right, dear,"
she said. "I've had a *very*
restful day and I'm feeling
much better now. Why don't
you all join me for a snack?"

"Well, if you're *sure,*" said Mr. Large, and everyone piled onto the bed to tell Mrs. Large all about the day she'd missed.

The End

Jill Murphy has written and illustrated several award-winning picture books, including *All In One Piece*, which was Highly Commended for the Kate Greenaway Medal, and *Five Minutes' Peace*, about which *Publishers Weekly* said, "This book is pure joy, one that parents, not just children, will want to keep on hand; Murphy's frazzled mom will find a soft spot in every reader." Jill Murphy is also the author of the Worst Witch series, which has more than five million copies in print worldwide. She lives in Cornwall, England.